CANCER

JUNE 21 - JULY 22

baby

Look out, world !

A Cancer was born on _____.

What is my Cancer Baby destined to be?

Learn to trust your instincts.

Your intuition holds the key.

Cancerians are full of compassion,
a quality no one can deny.

Baby Cancer, you are known as
the caregiver of the zodiac,
so your nurturing nature will be hard to hide.

Do you know you are a water sign?

Feelings can ebb and flow like the tide.

Yes, you have a protective shell,

but you'll learn to show your soft side.

As a homebody at heart,

you'll turn your home into a cozy retreat.

You'll fill it with warmth and comfort
and the smell of a freshly baked treat.

When counting your blessings,

family and friends

are the main things that you treasure.

Baby Cancer,
you are loyal beyond belief and loved beyond measure.

With your kind and generous heart,
you can brighten anyone's day.

You can achieve anything you want.

Let the light within you lead the way.

About the Author

Jen Neary is a Sagittarius
who always felt like she was destined
to be a writer. As the only fire sign in her family,
she was inspired to create this modern
zodiac baby book series for parents and
guardians to learn more about their child's
character traits and unique greatness.

CPSIA information can be obtained
at www.ICGtesting.com
Printed in the USA
JSHW041401100523
41166JS00005B/4